Bilingual Books Collection

California Immigrant Alliance Project

Funded by
The California State Library

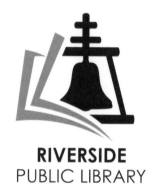

RIVERSIDE
PUBLIC LIBRARY

Es hora de... / It's Time

Es hora de cortarse el pelo
It's Time for a Haircut

Cathryn Summers

traducido por / translated by Charlotte Bockman

ilustrado por / illustrated by
Aurora Aguilera

PowerKiDS
press.

New York

Published in 2018 by The Rosen Publishing Group, Inc.
29 East 21st Street, New York, NY 10010

First Edition

Translator: Charlotte Bockman
Editorial Director, Spanish: Nathalie Beullens-Maoui
Editor, Spanish: Rossana Zúñiga
Editor, English: Elizabeth Krajnik
Art Director: Michael Flynn
Book Design: Raúl Rodriguez
Illustrator: Aurora Aguilera

Cataloging-in-Publication Data

Names: Summers, Cathryn, author.
Title: It's time for a haircut = Es hora de cortarse el pelo / Cathryn Summers.
Description: New York : PowerKids Press, [2018] | Series: It's time = La hora de... | In English and Spanish. Includes index.
Identifiers: ISBN 9781508163626 (library bound book)
Subjects: LCSH: Haircutting–Juvenile literature.
Classification: LCC TT970 .S86 2018 | DDC 646.7/24–dc23

Manufactured in the United States of America

CPSIA Compliance Information: Batch #BW18PK. For further information contact Rosen Publishing, New York, New York at 1-800-237-9932.

Contenido

Contents

4

Hoy es un día especial. ¡Me voy a ir a cortar el pelo por primera vez!

Today is a special day. I'm going to get my first haircut!

Mi papá y yo vamos en auto a la peluquería.

My dad and I drive to the barbershop.

El peluquero primero le corta el pelo a mi papá.

The barber cuts my dad's hair first.

Hay muchos señores
en la peluquería.
Están conversando.

There are a lot of men in the barbershop.

They talk to each other.

Ahora es mi turno. ¡Estoy muy emocionado
de que me corten el pelo!

Now it's my turn. I'm very excited for my haircut!

El peluquero primero usa las tijeras.

Me corta mucho pelo.

First, the barber uses scissors. He cuts off lots of hair.

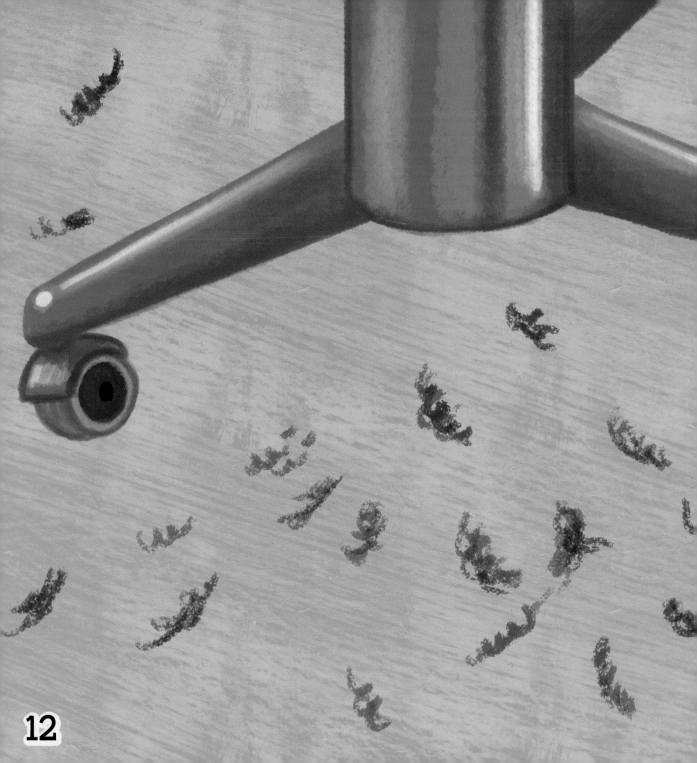

12

Me gusta ver como cae mi pelo al piso.

¡Mi pelo va a quedar corto!

I like to see my hair drop on the floor.

My hair is going to be short!

Después, el peluquero usa la máquina de afeitar. La máquina deja mi pelo muy corto.

Next, the barber uses the clippers. These cut my hair very short.

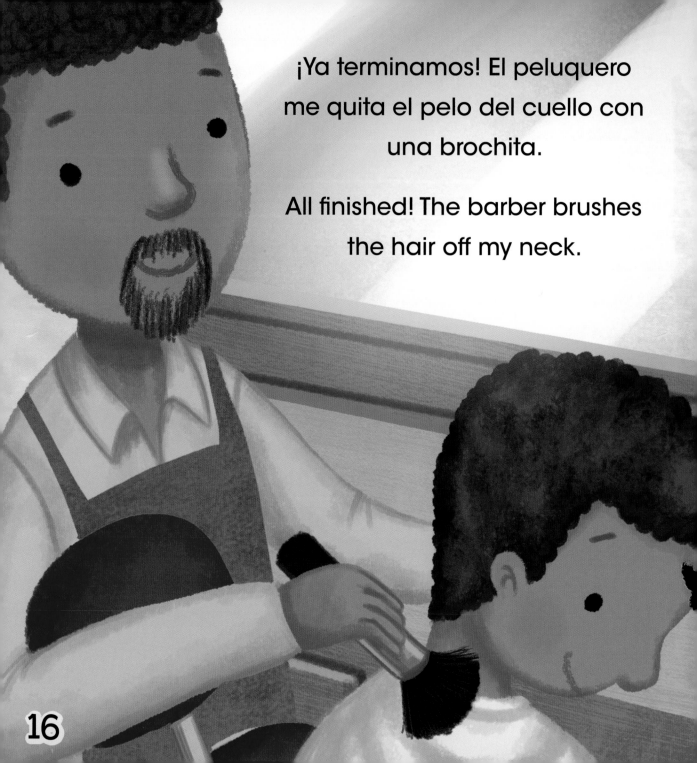

¡Ya terminamos! El peluquero me quita el pelo del cuello con una brochita.

All finished! The barber brushes the hair off my neck.

16

¡Guau! ¡Mi corte de pelo se ve muy bien!
Le doy las gracias al peluquero.

Wow! My haircut looks great!
I say thank you to the barber.

Mi papá le paga al peluquero.

¡Nos gusta cortarnos el pelo!

My dad pays the barber.
We like getting
our hair cut!

21

A mi mamá le gusta mucho mi corte de pelo. ¡Ya quiero volver a cortármelo!

My mom loves my haircut.
I can't wait for
the next one!

23

Palabras que debes aprender
Words to Know

(el) peluquero
barber

(la) máquina
de afeitar

clippers

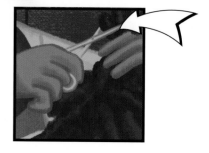

(las) tijeras
scissors

Índice / Index

24